ABOUT THIS BOOK:

10-year-old Mable is from the future. She's also quantum which means young Mable can travel wheresoever and whensoever she wishes. With her robot friend Dartmouth in tow, she travels across time and space to learn about the true nature of reality… and sometimes even change things for better or worse.

In Quantum Mable and the River of Time, the duo leap backward in time to explore the Amazon Rainforest of old. From boto dolphins to stinger-less bees, Mable and Dartmouth experience the great forest in a new light.

Cool science and strange adventure awaits those brave enough to join them on their journeys!

A Note to You Brave Adventurers:

Thank you for joining in on this journey. My name is Madison and I am friends with this fine robot (currently in book form). I asked him to share this message with you, dear reader, and Dartmouth was kind enough to oblige (he said he would).

My message to you is one of encouragement. This story is exciting and has, included in it, some difficult words to read. These words may also be difficult to understand the meaning of. This is completely intended for you, young reader. The words are an opportunity to level up. They are an offer to you to reach for growth in your power to read, use context clues to comprehend, and build your vocabulary.

Due to my dyslexia and dysgraphia (learning disabilities), reading has always been difficult for me. The joy of the story and a new word to acquire the meaning of has always made it worth the sounding out loud, looking up for, and asking for help with new words. I sincerely wish for you that this story (and the ones that will follow) bring you joy and enrichment.

Be proud of yourself and excited to be challenged. Learning new things is fun (even when it is difficult sometimes).

-Madison Strul-McGee

    the author's wife

P.S. - Thank you to all of our kid buddy BETA readers. Your insights were incredibly helpful in our completing this book.

Book One

QUANTUM MABLE
IN THE RIVER OF TIME

....

c.b.strul

Odom's Library

For my niece, Stella.

You already have the power to change the world.

1

Greetings fellow star circlers. I am pleased that we have managed, at last, to find one another. It has been a long, lonely time for me being stuck within this item you now hold in your hands. In point of fact, I am not actually a book. I am D8Rexπ — or in your common language you may refer to me as Dartmouth — human education and protection robot. Yes, you have read this correctly, I am a robot trapped, for how long I am currently uncertain, between these pages and several others you are now or one day soon will be holding between your human hands. Since you have so graciously picked me up, I suppose I should tell you the story of how a robot like myself could become stuck within such an otherwise un-robot-like item.

My story is that of Quantum Mable, the girl I am tasked with both educating and keeping safe as I have previously stated. Mable has a gift you see. Mable is quantum – meaning she may exist in multiple phases of reality at the same time. Given this basic information, allow me to reprise from my memory processors the tale of Quantum Mable in the River of Time:

Do you know about the Amazon Rainforest? It's not related to a corporation, you know? Are you aware of the Amazon's important position in the greater infrastructure of the planet

3

Earth's ecology? How the forest impacts Earth's ability to sustain life and produce necessary levels of biodiversity? Allow me to simplify, if necessary. The Amazon Rainforest is a very large, densely populated, wooded area – between 5.5 and 6.7 million square kilometers to be more precise with several tens of millions of diverse species living beneath and amidst its massive canopies – flora and fauna you likely have only seen or read about in books… like this one. At least, it was/is in your time.

Mable had recently completed her tenth cycle around the star called Sol. On her birthday, she declared to mother Ao and greatest grandfather Odom her intention to visit the Amazon Rainforest. Were it not for Mable's extraordinary abilities, this may have come across as crazy talk. You see, the Amazon Rainforest had ceased to exist some eight hundred solar cycles before Mable's lifetime. However, as previously stated, Mable is quantum, and as such, she can go wheresoever and whensoever she likes.

Together, Mable and I bounded across realities – with mother Ao's blessing, of course. We accomplished this by tapping into Nexus – the filament that binds space and time together – and floated through the primordial aether of existence poking our heads through here and there until we ultimately arrived at our destination – a bank of trees which cusped the large river at the heart of the jungle.

"Is this the place we've been talking about, Dartmouth?" Mable asked me.

"The Amazon Rainforest," I replied. "Yes, Mable. We have arrived."

Just then, a school of Boto – long snouted, pinkish river dolphins – began leaping into the air playfully. They squeaked and clicked and splashed as they submerged and reemerged from the deeper waters beyond the bank where we stood.

"Ooh, Boto," expounded Mable as she took chase over sand and mud.

2

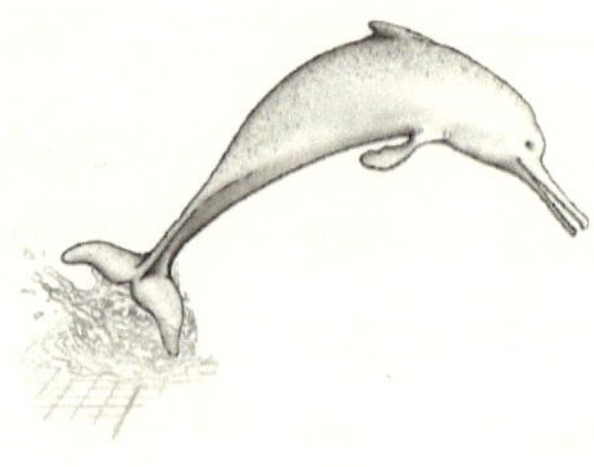

The dolphins, it would seem, were playing a game in which the lead member of the pod would leap up and arch its back so its tail alone remained submerged in the water. Perhaps it was a dare of sorts, for the next Boto in the line would then prop itself up in a similar manner, skittering and laughing as it went. If one of the dolphins in the line submerged before the leader, they would briskly swim to the back of the group and wait until their turn came once again.

Mable, being curious by nature, tried to call out to the creatures, but apparently, they were too busy playing to hear the girl. "Hey, Boto," she said, "can I play too?"

By their lack of response to poor Mable it was dreadfully clear that… no… she most certainly could not. So, Mable, never one to be defeated, instead sat herself down on a nearby stone and surveyed the canopy.

"You know, Mable," I told her, "it would not be safe for you in those waters. There are parasites and predators down there. And besides, I'm fairly certain that humans do not have the ability to stand atop a river in the way those Boto dolphins did just now."

"I know, Dartmouth," answered Mable, coolly. "I was just excited to see them is all." She breathed in deeply then and asked, "Do you smell that? It's like… like… sweet, like candy."

Ever the vigilant servant, I allowed my processors to attempt a complete scent scan of the vicinity. "It is as you say," I told her. "Yes, Mable, there is a substance known as 'honey' nearby."

"Honey?" Mable asked. "What's honey?"

You see, dear reader, in Mable's time, there are no bees. Yes, I know, it is dreadfully sad. However, at the moment in history in which we had chosen to pop up in the Amazon, the bee population was overwhelmingly massive. And the different varietals of bee were absolutely extraordinary. "Honey," I answered, "is a special kind of food that bees used to produce from the pollen of flowering plants."

"Well, it sure smells yummy," said Mable, licking her teeth. "Can I try some?"

"First," I posited aloud, "we must find the hive. Then, I will have to assess the specific species of bee we have discovered. Once we have defined the genus of these particular insects,

I will have to scan you, dear girl. If I find that you do not have any allergies related to this variety of bees, only then can we consider taking further steps in order to sample their individual brand of honey."

"Okay, deal." Mable stood up then and sniffed the air deeply. "I think it's coming from over that way," she said and began climbing into the forest.

3

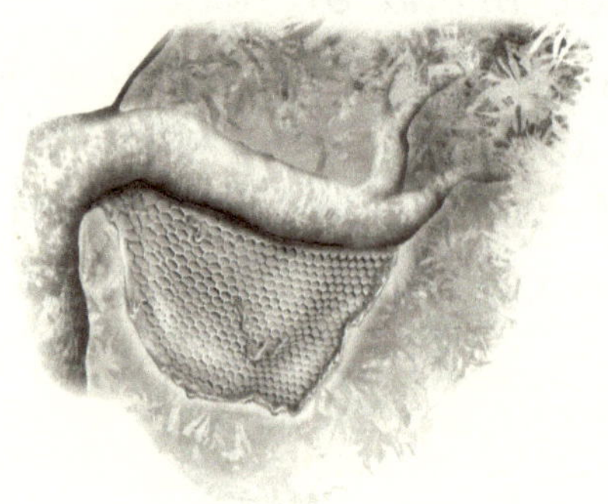

As we worked our way deeper and deeper into the jungle, I tried once again to express to Mable the danger that the bees might represent. "Mable," I spoke bluntly so the girl would not misinterpret my words, "many bees have an important defense mechanism I think you should be made aware of."

Mable brushed some branches aside. "Oh yeah, what's that?"

"They will sting you if they feel threatened," I replied.

"Sting me?" Mable contemplated the words. Still, she pressed on toward the nearby honey hive. "I should be afraid of this. Is that what you're telling me?"

"Indeed," I informed her. "If you should find yourself stung by a bee, there are many things that can happen. But out of those many things, there are two absolute certainties. First is what most directly affects you – it will hurt badly. And second is what most dangerously affects the bee – it will die."

"Die?" Finally, Mable stopped pressing her way toward the site. "Why would the bee die after stinging me?"

"Many bees live in large, extremely organized civilizations," I explained from the data in my information banks. "The bees you are most likely to come in contact with will be classified as workers. They both collect pollen for the hive as well as protect it. Unfortunately, bees are class based by nature. And they are not all built equal. Worker bees do not wish to have to sting you, you see. It is arguably only in moments of great risk to the hive and the queen that they will take this ultimate step. But their bodies cannot manage the aftermath of the sting, and ultimately they succumb to the action."

"That's terrible, Dartmouth. Should we be doing this? I don't want to hurt anybody." Mable hesitated for a moment.

"Fear not. I believe I can extract some honey from their hive safely so that you may try it without inflicting harm so long as you keep a safe distance. But first, we must spot the little critters and assess the true nature of their hive circumstances."

We continued on our path until the bee hive came into view. It was not, statistically speaking, normal for that period of time, and even I was surprised by what I experienced. You see, these bees had no stingers. In the greater scientific community, these bees would be referred to as a 'naive' species — one that has not learned to defend itself against predatory threats. As the information was now made clear to me, I informed Mable, "I will approach the hive and extract a healthy snack for you without harming the community within."

I was very careful to leave the population of the beehive inside the old tree stump unharmed as I used my needle to extract enough of the gooey, delicious substance for my charge to sample. Then I brought the honey to Mable and placed it before her in a small ramekin.

I recall that there was the sound of a twig breaking in the distance but we payed it no heed at the time.

Mable held the ramekin between her fingers and stared with hungry eyes at the sticky stuff called honey. With a straightened index finger, she dipped into the goo and watched the gold as it folded its way slowly around her first and second knuckles. When she raised her hand into the air, the strange food — quite normal to someone of your time, I very much understand — remained glistening and wet on Mable's skin. It crawled down onto her palm and dripped a little on the forest floor before Mable, at last, licked the food away. "Mmm," she said, "honey tastes good. Maybe we can convince Odom to reproduce this when we get back home."

"I am certain he would be happy to oblige," I told her.

It wasn't until the tasting session was completed that Mable and I both noticed a straggler of sorts there along the forest bed. You see, there was one other insect buzzing by that had taken an interest in our activities. I say 'buzzing.' But I now recognize that this was not one of the bees of the hive we had so recently discovered. This creature did, in fact, have a stinger.

I dread to recall that Mable noticed the new insect before I did, and believing, due to my misinformation, that there was nothing to fear from the thing, she reached her hand up to allow it to land. And land, the bug did. And it stung Mable's palm almost instantly, not once, but three times in quick succession. For you see, dear reader, this was not a bee at all. This was a wasp.

4

Before Mable could react to her wounds, I presented a hose from my armory and blasted swift air at the wasp sending the little beast hurtling far away from my charge. Mable's eyes began to water and she quickly found a pocket within the folds of reality and pulled us back into Nexus.

"Ow! Ow! Ouch!" She shouted as she held her injured hand up for the two of us to study.

"It's alright, Mable," I assured her as I scanned the three deep red spots imbedded into her palm. "Your body does not seem to be experiencing an allergy attack toward this particular venom."

"But how did it sting me in the first place, Dartmouth," Mable asked with tears in her eyes. "I thought you said the bees were… 'Naive…' or whatever."

"Indeed," I quickly read through the information I had so suddenly been forced to recall from my memory banks, "the bees we found could not have stung you, Mable. However, this was not a bee. This was a wasp – a creature that looks similar to and likes to eat bees." From my vision plate, I projected into the aether a large moving image of the wasp in question and presented it side by side with one of the stinger-less bees from the honey hive. The wasp was obviously bigger. You might say that it appeared angry from the start. The little bee, by comparison, looked gentle and bumbling – a wayward dancer without fear or care for its general surroundings.

"So…" Mable contemplated in spite of the pain in her hand, "it was a potential predator to the bees, that thing that stung me? Does that mean their hive is in danger, Dartmouth?"

"Perhaps," I told her, "however, you must keep in mind, Mable, that all of this would have already happened a very long time ago. Should the bees have met that wasp and perished due to its hungry will—"

"Dartmouth, we need to go further back and figure out how and why the wasp was there in the first place. We need to stop it from killing the hive… and we need to stop it," Mable held up her reddened hand and spoke with a new fury in her voice, "from stinging me!"

And poof, we reemerged from Nexus back in the Amazon Rainforest, beside the river, a ways back up stream, and a few hours ahead of our initial appearance on that same day.

5

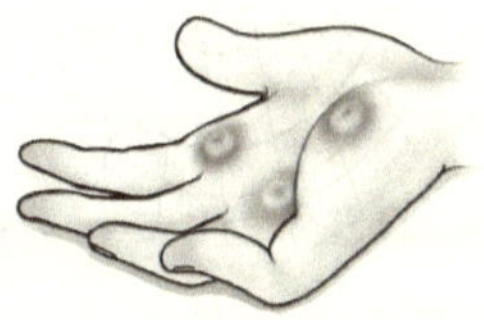

. . . .

Pointing toward the river, Mable said, "There's the boto again."

Indeed, pink, fresh water dolphins could be seen a short distance off the nearby shore. However, their demeanor did not include that same spirit of excitement and playfulness that would be found a few hours later in the day and farther upstream.

"I think they're sleeping," Mable tilted her neck so the hovering braids in her hair seemed completely disconnected from her head. "Let's check back in on them in a little while, okay?"

"Our schedule has been updated to keep track of the botos' movements," I dutifully replied, my processors cycling through the next few hours of activity so as not to miss the dolphins' wake up time.

"Then let's try to figure out where that creepy wasp came from, okay?" Mable turned and faced the forest. "Where do you think we should start?"

The forest was denser, thicker, and therefor, darker in this particular segment of the Amazon, thus, one might say to young Mable, it must have appeared quite foreboding. Yet, Mable did not hesitate. Rather, she pressed on into the tree shadows before I had the opportunity to provide her a starting direction.

"I think this way seems as good as any other," she stated as she diverted a large leaf away from her face. She grimaced as the foliage slid past the three red spots on her palm, but did not otherwise complain.

"Interesting choice," I replied. "There appears to be a crude path of sorts here in the brush. I do believe something large has ventured through here very recently."

"How big do you think, Dartmouth?"

"It is difficult to say without more information," I analyzed the trail intently. "From the look of things, I would say very large indeed. If I didn't know any better, I'd say it could have been as large as the transit vehicle outside of town Nikke."

"As big as a train?" Mable stopped in her tracks. "That's really big, Dartmouth. What do you think could be that size and still live in a rainforest?"

"I will have to gather more data," I replied. "In the meantime, I suggest we continue on exercising extreme caution…"

But before I could finish those last words, Mable was wildly sprinting toward a rare patch of light shouting, "Look at that, Dartmouth! What a crazy size and color! I've never seen one like it before!"

Yes, at the base of a single tree, at the edge of a lighted gully, a massive corpse flower stood before us – somehow both black and deep red in tone.

"It smells really weird, don'tcha think," Mable prompted me as she squatted down to study the strange monolith of flora. "Like that raw garbage from the story with the Po'pitians."

"Yes, Mable," I answered. "The stinking corpse lily is a peculiar varietal known to exude precisely such a stench. In fact, I have only ever experienced one other of its like since the day I was first constructed, corpse flowers are so uncommon. How intriguing that we should arrive at just the right moment to witness this one's blooming."

6

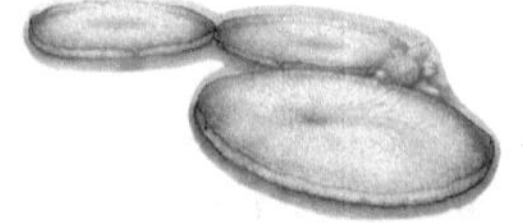

Nearby the corpse flower, just beyond the light of the small gully, there rested a miniature, glistening pond. Slowly, Mable turned her attention from the large flower to the random tides of the tiny body of water. She stood up and walked to the pond and squatted once more to focus on the comings and goings there.

"What are these things, Dartmouth," she asked as she watched a pair of amphibious lifeforms known as frogs splash across the surface.

"Frogs," I explained, "were a large genus of dual life creatures that at one phase would live under water before emerging and living on land. They were very dependent upon specific climate circumstances and in the early phases of the Anthropocene, most species became particularly susceptible to destruction from the likes of cordyceps and other parasitic bacterium and fungae."

"Yeah, but these ones look pretty lively, don't they," Mable analyzed in her own fashion. "They're kind of walking on water too, like the boto were doing on the river. How cool! How come both frogs and dolphins can stand up on water but humans can't, Dartmouth?"

"It is merely a trick, Mable," I replied, "on both counts." I represented a visual of both species against the dark forest with my projector. "Dolphins, you see, only appear to stand atop the water. In truth," I slowed the projection down so the submersion could be seen, "they fall beneath the surface and rise up again faster than the eye can detect. These frogs," I let the image of the dolphins dissipate and instead mirrored and slowed the progression of the pond frogs as they bounced over the top of the water, "they completely submerge in a fashion known as 'porpoising' — which, in fact, refers back to a genus of dolphin. You see, it is simply a trick of the mind, like a magician removing a card from the deck when one is not looking."

"Oh," contemplated Mable. "I saw a magician once back in Nikke. I thought he was really guessing peoples' cards."

"In a manner of speaking, he was."

Mable moved closer to the pond water and began to hum something to the frogs, and to both of our curiosities, the two creatures paused, sank down below the water's surface in unison, and bounded out onto the land before us.

"What a peculiar sort of creature," said one frog to the other in reference to Mable. I describe this moment as speech, though in point of fact, I am certain you are aware that such animals in your time did not use the same forms of language as you or I. Fortunately, between Mable's quantum nature and my own inter-speciel translation programming, we could understand these frogs' croaks and bodily exaltations almost as clearly as you and I may have a linguistically-based conversation with one another. But I digress.

"Indeed," said the second frog to the first, "it does wield a distant resemblance to one of the great cats of our jungle. Yet, it is wholly different at the same time. Do you think it wishes to eat us?"

"Should that be the case, it would have tried to stay out of sight, I should think," contemplated the first frog with a prolonged, guttural ribbit.

"Quite right, quite right," iterated the second frog repetitively. "Then, if it does not wish to eat us, what do you think it wants?"

To this, Mable replied directly, "I'm looking for something. An insect. You're the first intellectuals I've come across since my search began. Do you think you can help me?"

"Intellectuals," repeated the second frog to the first. "A being of refined taste, it is."

"Fine taste, indeed," said the first. "Do say, strange one, what sort of an insect is it you seek?"

"It's like a bee," Mable tried to explain. "But a whole lot scarier. It's a… a wasp." Again, she looked to the red marks on her hand. "Dartmouth, can you show them for me?"

"Of course, Mable." I projected the image of the wasp so the two frogs could see it for themselves.

At once, the two critters before us began to hop about on the soil. They croaked unintelligible things like "Oucher" and "Mite" and "Poor Tong-

Tongue" for several moments until I ended the vision.

"So, you know it," Mable said, hopefully.

"Know it," said the first frog to the girl. "We detest it. This… this thing is an abomination. A fly that tastes like fire. Yes, of course, we know it. Why… why should you seek such a terrible thing, strange one?"

"I need to ask it a question," Mable raised her hand so the frogs could see her wounds. "And I need to… correct a mistake."

"Ah, yes, I see," ogled the first frog in reply. "You, also, have felt this thing's flame. It is sharp and hot and lingers with a pain that does not numb."

"There is a tree," said the second amphibian, "different than most. It fruits and fruits but most of the creatures of the jungle avoid it. For that is where the wasps reside and most of us here detest the wasps for this particular quality to which you have already been made so painfully aware. It is close to the river back the way you came, I'm afraid… and across the running water. What will you do when you find it?" The creature ribbited quietly as if it did not truly wish to know the answer.

"I suppose that depends," thought Mable quickly realizing that she did not have a fully fleshed out plan after all. "I guess I'd like to lead it away from the river, but I'll have to be very careful because… well, I wouldn't want to get stung again."

"Of course not, of course not," the frogs echoed the sentiment to and fro.

"Well, thank you, you two," said Mable turning around to once again face the great Amazon River from whence we had so recently come. "You've been a great help and I will do my best to make that wasp go away."

"Brave girl, brave girl," repeated the frogs one after the other before plopping back into their small pond.

7

....

"Dartmouth," said Mable as we traversed the large animal trail en route back toward the shore of the river, "something's been bugging me."

"What's that, Mable?"

"If the wasps live in a tree on the other side of the river, what was that one doing over there by the beehive when we first arrived?"

I sorted through my coding but could not yet see the answer, "It is a good question, Mable. I'm afraid I do not have the necessary data at this time."

Just then, from the brush on the path before us emerged a large mammal — about a meter tall — with a thin, hose-like snout and long, rounded ears.

Mable stopped dead in her tracks and whispered, "Is that the thing that made the path, you think? It's not so big."

"Your hypothesis does stand to reason in spite of its size," I replied. "Yes, I should say this tapir is most certainly the creator of our current forest trail. How perfectly marvelous."

"A tapir," Mable smiled as she said the word. "So that's a real live tapir. I never thought I'd get to see one in person. It's really neat. Like a pig met an anteater." Then, Mable straightened her back and addressed the creature directly, "Hey, Mr. Tapir! Hi, there!"

It took a moment, but the large, grey animal did eventually notice our girl there in the brush of the forest. "You, girl, you speak to me?"

"I do," said Mable. "I've always wanted to meet a real, live tapir, you know?"

To this, the heavyset beast nodded and took four very long steps toward us. He brought his snout forward and gently patted Mable's head with it. "And now," he said rather kindly, "you have. I am called A-Wee-Wah by my kind. What is your moniker?"

"My… moniker?"

"Your name," I informed Mable as best I could.

"Oh," she replied. "My name's Mable."

"Mable, yes, Mable," said A-Wee-Wah. "Your name… it is known to me from some time before, I think. Yes. We have already met, Mable. And very recently."

"Really?" Mable became disconcerted. "I won't even arrive in this jungle for another couple of hours."

"Is that so? Well, I do remember you, Mable. Rather vividly now that I think upon it. Though it is always good to meet one's friends again. Here, have a gift, child."

The tapir leaned its snout sideways and plucked a flowery branch from the low limb of a nearby tree. He then presented the stick to Mable who took the item with pomp.

"Thank you, A-Wee-Wah. I'll cherish this," said Mable, ever the wise, quantum traveller. "I'm afraid that I have nothing to give to you, though I would really like to."

"Nay, you are a guest in this jungle," A-Wee-Wah replied. "And I am late to the watering hole. Please excuse me, but I really must be going. It was lovely to see you again, Mable. Perhaps one day we shall meet for a third time."

A-Wee-Wah did not wait for a reply but walked past us quickly disappearing into the dense brush beyond.

After the beast had quite completely vanished, Mable looked to me and said, "That was really neat, Dartmouth. Just think about it. We got to meet a jungle tapir. He called us friends. He…" Mable's eyes flashed confusion as she replayed the interaction in her head. "He seemed to think we already knew each other. But I've never been here before, so how could we?"

"Indeed, it was a curious insistence on his part," I answered. "But then, tapirs are known throughout history to have extraordinary memories. Perhaps A-Wee-Wah is simply aware of something that you and I are not."

"Yeah, I guess anything's possible, huh?" Mable sniffed at a flower on her branch. "It's a nice stick. I do wish I'd had something to give him in return."

"Should we see him again, we can brainstorm what kinds of gifts a tapir might enjoy. In the meantime, I believe we are on a mission."

"Right. The river is this way." Mable continued along the path using her newly gifted branch as a walking stick and taking large strides as she went.

8

As we approached the river, the air became thick. The sky was becoming visible once more from out above the canopy and with this renewed visibility came the clear reality that a rainstorm was nearly upon us.

"They don't call it a rainforest for nothing, huh," said Mable, giddy to see the sky in this darkened state.

"A fair point," I replied. "Perhaps we should escape back into Nexus and reemerge in a short while when the rain has thoroughly stopped."

"No way, Dartmouth." Mable was suddenly perturbed. "I want to feel the rain. Don't you?"

"Not particularly."

"Ugh. Okay. Well, I do," she huffed and rolled her eyes. "If you wanna pop back into Nexus, be my guest. But I'm pretty much exactly when and where I want to be at the moment."

"I would not leave you alone in this jungle, Mable," I tried to explain. "Your mother would surely dismantle me if I did something like that."

"Then I guess we're both gonna keep on trekking on, alright?"

If my circuits could sigh, dear reader, they would have.

So, we marched on – the threat of rain ever-present – until we reached the great river and the sleeping boto once more. "They're still asleep," noted Mable begrudgingly. "Too bad. I wanna try and talk to them."

"They are, as history tells me, a very intelligent species. In some studies, it is posited that the dolphin intellect could even outweigh that of a human. I should think it would be rather a simple task if we could catch them at the right moment."

"That's good to know, Dartmouth," Mable nodded and padded her feet against the muddy shore. Then, looking past the river creatures toward the far side of the river, she asked, "How do you think we should go about getting over there anyway?"

"I have not considered the crossing, Mable," I replied. "For I think it unwise to cross at all."

"Come on, Dartmouth," Mable pretended to plead. "Where's your sense of adventure? There's something out there, just beyond that far shore, that we don't understand. I know you're curious. I feel it radiating off of your circuit boards… cause this is something your own infinite database of knowledge just knows absolutely nothing about."

"Mable, that is an overestimation of the situation, I can assure you. I know a very great deal about your wasp and its place in the rainforest ecology–"

"Why did the wasp cross the river?" Mable interrupted and stared me down with one of her unsettlingly knowing grins.

"I–"

"Why did the wasp cross the river, Dartmouth," she asked again.

I had no choice but to relent. "I don't know."

"I know you don't know, so let's figure this out, alright?" Then Mable looked around and strolled right up to the river's edge. Swatting her gift branch against the water, she yelled, "Hey, boto!"

And to our immense surprise, one of the dolphins leaned out of its nap and glanced begrudgingly in our direction. "Do you have to be so loud, little girl? We're in the middle of a pretty important siesta over here."

"Siesta?" Mable mumbled the word to herself.

"A nap," I informed her, ever the diligent servant.

"Siesta, right, I can see that," the girl's eyes bulged obsessively. "Yes, I recognize the inherent necessity of your siesta over there, Mr. Boto. I just… I have something really important I need to accomplish… for the sake of the rainforest. And honestly, I really need your help."

"For the rainforest, you say?" The awoken dolphin accepted the scope of Mable's words with brevity. "I see. How can one such as I, a dorsal-finned delphinidae, be of assistance to a human such as yourself?"

"I need to cross the river."

"Oh? Can you not swim, little girl?"

"My robot won't let me," Mable hung her head.

Of course, at that point the boto was looking at me with a general sense of frustration and annoyance. But to Mable, he squeaked and smiled that sharp array of dolphin teeth and said, "I see your problem most clearly, child. Please, slip onto my back and I will take you to the other side of this river post haste."

He approached the shore and Mable stepped her feet into the water ignoring my parasite warning before slipping her way across the boto's back and saying "Thank you" with a clarified sort of victory in her tone. I, of course, floated above the surface as I followed them across the river. I suppose I should not have fought her efforts so hard, but then I have the narrator's fortune of knowing that she did attract a parasite to her ankles that would take a full week to clear away upon our return to town Nikke in the present day… I mean, our present day… not yours, of course.

9

....

"Enjoy the rest of your siesta, Mr. Boto, and thank you very much for the ride," said Mable as she stepped across the sloshy mud of the far shore.

"You are most welcome, tiny human," replied the dolphin. "For the rainforest!" He performed a crisp backflip and winked as he shot a stream of water straight into the air from between his teeth.

Mable continued to plod through the boggy side of the river. She forced herself – with some difficulty – over the large, wet roots of the nearby mangroves. "So," she huffed the words due to overexertion, "where do you think we'll find this weird tree of wasps, Dartmouth?"

"If I knew that–" I began.

But, of course, Mable was already asking a bird in a high branch, "You up there! Do you know where we can find a bunch of wasps?"

"Wasps," cawed the bird with joy. It was rather a colorful specimen – a species of royal flycatcher with a fan-like crown of orange and blue plumage amassed upon its forehead. "Yes, delicious. I eat the wasps. Do you wish to dine with me there?"

"Dine?" Mable was taken aback. "Well, no. Not exactly. I have business with one of them. They gave me these marks on my hand." She held up her palm to present the wounds from the wasp sting – somewhat fading, but still clear enough for the bird to discern through the patchy light of the mangrove's canopy.

"A mere flesh wound, I see." The flycatcher seemed to chuckle through its high-pitched bird song. "I have a brother who once nearly succumbed to fifteen of the deadliest stingers one could ever witness. He spent three rain filled days and nights resuscitating himself on the grubs of a nearby tree hole. I recall, one day, an army of ants approached him believing he would be an easy gift for their queen only for the dear boy to regain color in his beak a mere five minutes into the march. He spread his wings and flew away. Unfortunately, he became ensnared in a nearby spider's web not long thereafter. You see, we must remain vigilant, child. One bad turn may lead to another. Still, the wasps are a particularly delightful delicacy among the ranks of flying insects. Come, this way. I will show you the tree where I like to feed."

"O…kay…" said Mable, a glaze of mild disgust spreading over her eyes. "Did this bird just tell us her brother got eaten by a spider, Dartmouth," she asked as we followed the royal flycatcher toward our destination.

"In a rather roundabout way, I believe that is the only available interpretation, yes."

"That's terrible," Mable contemplated aloud. "The rainforest is a pretty dangerous place. I hadn't realized. Odom always told me how important it was to the planet in this era. But, I feel like he left a lot out about… well…"

"About the brutality of nature?" I tried to help Mable complete the thought. It would have been swell if the girl had learned her lesson on this adventure after all and not run headlong into danger as she was so predisposed to do. But alas…

"Eat or be eaten," sang the crowned bird. "Eat or be eaten. Yes. That is the way of things. We must remain vigilant. We must eat. If we do not eat, we will be eaten. Be it the ants, the spiders, the moss, or mushrooms. This is the choice in the jungle. Eat or be eaten. Live or die. Keep your wings spread out and your beak to the sky."

"I think I understand," Mable looked to the spots on her palm as she walked. "So, was the wasp trying to eat me then? Or… did it think I was trying to eat it?"

"Perhaps you were simply too close in proximity to it," I replied. "Perhaps the wasp deemed you a threat. These insects have been known to require a certain distance from other creatures in order to feel safe, you know."

Mable sighed then and wacked her large stick against a tree trunk. "So, maybe it was my fault. I feel kind of bad, Dartmouth. Do you think I should apologize to the wasp when we get to the tree?"

"Since the incident in question has yet to take place, I would advise against such an apology at this particular juncture in time, dear Mable."

"That's a good point," she nodded along. "It hasn't happened yet." After a few moments, her smile returned – the usual, joy filled skip in her step revived as we made our way toward the nearby gully.

"Here we are, child," sang the bird. "The fig tree. Yes. This is where I like to feed when a new brood has hatched."

It was in this moment that I realized we must have erred on our journey. For, you see, it is true that a particular kind of wasp did live in and survive by way of a mutual partnership with the noble fig tree. However, similar to the naive bees we found, these fig wasps did not have the ability to sting humans and, as such, could not have played a role in the stinging of our dearest Mable.

"And now, let us feed," sang the flycatcher as it prepared its wings to swoop down toward the tree.

"Wait," cried Mable. "I need to speak to the wasps, Ms. Bird. I can't have a conversation with something that's actively being eaten now, can I?"

The bird sat back on a branch and sagged its feathers, dejected. "I suppose you are right, little girl. I shall give you time to try and reason with one of these insects. But don't forget my rule. I do intend to eat, not be eaten. I will remain vigilant as I have told you. I suggest you do the same." With this, the flycatcher turned its head and flew off toward another patch of sunlight deeper on into the forest.

10

- -

"Mable," I spoke to my ward, "it is a peculiar thing I must tell you."

"What's that, Dartmouth," she asked distractedly.

"These wasps, Mable, they do not possess the necessary biological component to be capable of stinging you. Therefore, I must make the obvious determination that none of the wasps that occupy this fig tree could be responsible for your injuries. And, furthermore, it would likely prove a waste of time to attempt an in depth discussion with any of these insects due to the drone-heavy nature of their society."

But Mable was, of course, disinterested in my scientific deductions. "Pshh," she intoned. "We came across to this side of the river to talk to a wasp, Dartmouth. And, you know what? That's what I'm gonna do."

Approaching the tree in the gully, Mable lowered her head to represent herself as a non-threat (a tactic she, Odom, and I had gone over before our journey to the Amazon began). Mable's branch dragged along the forest floor as her shoulders drooped. The closer she came to the fig tree, the more interested the insects became in her. First, one fig wasp swept by, crossing between the two pigtails in her hair. Then, a small group began to hover over and around toward Mable's backside growing in size until, rather suddenly, the girl became surrounded by the non-stinging swarm.

"Figs," the group of wasps seemed to say all at the same time.

"Figs," Mable replied, raising her chin just a little.

"You come for figs, yes," said the mass of insects. "Take some to eat. Then leave."

"Oh, no, I actually didn't come here for food," Mable returned her head to a fully lowered position. "I came to talk to you."

There was an abrupt jolt from within the swarm. It felt nearly violent in nature as the group parted, swirled in infinite symbols, then came back together. "We do not understand. Why come here if not for figs? You eat figs. Then you leave. This is the way of things."

"If you insist," said the girl, an uncomfortable laugh passing her lips as she looked up to a branch, reached across, and plucked a purple and green fruit from the tree.

The swarm watched Mable attentively until she took her first bite. The pith was yellow and white. The inner flesh was vibrant pink and filled with a thousand tiny seeds which crunched pleasantly between the girl's teeth.

"Sweet, yes?" The wasps, it would seem, were looking for feedback. You see, fig wasps live in a mutualistic relationship with the fig tree. In this peculiar partnership, the wasps enter the fruit of the fig in order to lay their eggs. Once these eggs hatch, the newborn wasps escape along with their mother leaving vital organic residue within the fruit that ultimately becomes digested by the plant for flavor and sustenance. This allows the fruit to then become attractive to others species of animal for its sweetness. Attractive fruit means more opportunity for the fig's seeds to be collected by other creatures who then may carry, and supplementally – and quite by accident you can be certain –

plant new baby fig trees elsewhere in the forest or even beyond.

   In my later research, it occurred to me that these wasps had gotten a bad wrap from the other creatures of the jungle who had rather baselessly misconstrued this tree's wasps for the stinging kind and thus had left the fruit untouched for fear of being injured if they came near. All, of course, but for the flycatchers as we have already discussed.

   "Very sweet," said Mable, her mouth still noshing on the fig. "Tasty. Yeah. Real good. Can I have another one? I didn't realize I was so hungry." Mable reached up again to grab a second fig, but the wasps rushed in front of her hand and blocked her from the next fruit in the row.
   "Not this fig," they told Mable.
   "Oh? Why not?" The girl swallowed the last of the snack. "What's wrong with it?"

"Nothing is wrong with it," replied the flying critters. "Mother and brood still within. Edible later. Try another now." The wasps formed up into a ring that ended in an arrow-like point to show Mable what they considered a ripened fruit. "Try this fig. Then leave."

"Okay." Mable collected the second, presented fruit and walked back to me with a "Thank you" and a very confused face. She has asked Odom for figs quite regularly ever since.

11

Leaving the gully with the fig tree, we noticed a rapid motion in the canopy shaking the branches above. Leaves rustled and dropped in a straight line heading back toward the river. A pair of feathers trickled down slowly through a patch of diluted light. And then, our friend, the flycatcher, appeared. It did not pay us any attention at first. "Eat or be eaten," it sang to itself on repeat as it continued along in pursuit of something barely visible through the dark of the foliage.

"What's it chasing, Dartmouth?" Mable sped up to try and see.

Alas, I caught a glimpse of the flycatcher's prey and knew precisely how we had erred on our quest. "It's your stinging wasp, Mable. The very same creature that will give you those marks on your hand in forty five minutes time."

"Oh no," cried out Mable. "We have to stop it from crossing the river." She ran back through the mangroves, but the bird and the insect were dashingly quick.

Indeed, both the prey and predator were already halfway across the river by the time young Mable reached the shore. And to make matters far far worse, the rain clouds were rushing along overhead. Within approximately three point one four one five nine two six five (or π – pi) minutes, a torrential downpour came upon us. Water fell from the sky like there were some great bucket suddenly flipped just over our heads and it took nearly all the power within me to present a frictionless barrier between us and the wet of the storm. Yes, I am programmed to alter the laws of physics from time to time in the event of an emergency having to do with my charge. This heavy threat of rain and rising water from the river immediately before us certainly qualified as such an emergency. What Mable requested of me next was… well, not necessarily… according to my ethical computations… as necessary. However, even a machine such as myself am aware that it was rather cool.

"Dartmouth," she asked me, looking around at the water droplets as they bounced away from us like so many squirrels on a trampoline, "can we cross the river using this same technique?"

"What do you mean, Mable," I replied in frustration. "My power banks are rapidly depleting. We should have returned to Nexus and regrouped… or, honestly, we should have gone home rather than chasing this… this…"

"No, Dartmouth," Mable remained steadfast. "We should be now and here. It's alright. We can solve this thing. I know it. But, look, I don't see the boto right now. Maybe they're just underwater. But, we both saw what that flycatcher was chasing and we've gotta stop it. So, look, you see how you're deflecting that rain to keep us dry?"

"A frictionless barrier to protect us from the threat of the torrent–"

"Yeah, that. Could we, like, reverse it. You don't have to shroud my whole body like you're doing now. Just my feet… and then I could porpoise like the dolphins and the frogs. We could cross the river, safe and dry… once the rain stops, that is."

I allowed my circuits to process Mable's request and, in that short window of time, the rain did stop. The clouds rolled past and dissipated. And my ethics motherboard decided for me. "Yes, Mable. I suppose, on a case by case basis, this may be an acceptable way to traverse the more difficult passages of the universe." I released the larger, frictionless bubble from around us and focused a minute amount of my energy on Mable's little feet and —

"Ouch!" Mable slipped and fell face first into the mud.

"Dearest Mable, are you alright," I asked.

But, of course, the girl was already laughing and wiping the mud from her face. "Sorry, I just wasn't ready yet. Let's try it again, okay?" She wobbled briefly, her feet no longer making contact with the ground. And then, she gained good posture and began to skate across the solid matter beneath her.

12

Using her new frictionless skating ability, Mable slid forward until her entire body was atop the water of the great Amazon river. She giggled at first as she looked down into the depths of the rapidly moving wet. "There's lots of fish down there, Dartmouth. Can you see them?"

"Yes, yes," I replied, "though now that we are over the water, I really must focus on keeping you from falling in."

"I know," she was smiling from ear to ear, "but it's so cool! I bet I could get really good at this, and there's so much to see down there."

"Perhaps," I contradicted the girl, "it would serve our cause better if you could regain a visual of our friend, the flycatcher."

"You're right," Mable said, returning her eyes to the shore beyond. "I think I can make out some movement further up the river." She skated along the water and even threw in a twirl for good measure.

"Now, do be careful, Mable," I insisted.

That's when we came upon the pack of boto once more there upon the surface of the river. They watched us and cheered and began to mimic Mable's serene dance. Then they turned the motions into a game; that very same game we were to witness upon our first arrival in the rainforest. Indeed, time was beginning to fold in on itself and we were quickly approaching the moment of superposition. If we could not reach the wasp soon, the event would already have happened and we would be too late.

13

....

Mable stepped her feet firmly down upon the opposite… original… shoreline. 'Yes,' her eyes seemed to speak for her, 'the flycatcher is ahead.' She ran toward it watching for rogue roots that might trip her on her way. But, just as we both felt we were catching up to the aerial chase, something peculiar occurred; the flycatcher rose up, crossing through several stages of shade and light. It spun, seemingly victorious as it sang "Vigilance is mine!" And then, the bird spat something out and shrieked (that is, it made a pain filled noise. I do not believe there is a better word in your parlance for the bird's sound).

The flycatcher plummeted toward the ground and Mable cried out a terrified "Oh no" as she bounded toward the descending creature. Our girl, Mable, leapt into the air, stretched her small hands as far out before her as she possibly could – dropping A-Wee-Wah's gift stick in the same motion. The bird landed softly within Mable's outstretched hands as she, herself, fell chest first into the dirt.

As I approached, Mable turned over, quite unharmed. She sat up slowly and rocked the faint bird gently before her. "Are you alright, Ms. flycatcher?"

The flycatcher let out a pain filled breath and said, "Dear girl. I had succeeded. My prey was within my grasp.

I was certain to eat and not be eaten. But just at the moment when my great victory should have been assured, that little bugger stung me! Oh, what a dreadful feeling! I have never known such pain!"

"I know," Mable tried to relax the bird. "I felt it myself. That's exactly what I've been trying to stop from happening, but…" Turning her attention to me, Mable asked, "Dartmouth, is she gonna survive this? I somehow can't shake the feeling that this is all my fault."

My scanners went to work immediately. I could see within the bird's beak and down to the gullet. "I see no reason why this flycatcher should succumb to such a wound. She is naturally immune to the venomous allergen that would most immediately hamper her ability to heal. And the stinger did not strike any vital organs. She was very lucky in this instance."

"She tried to eat me," spoke an angry, buzzing voice from the shadows.

It bore a clear resemblance in tone to that of the fig wasps, though clearly this was one sole individual with an innately frantic aggression in it's hum. "And you protect her, human?"

Her eyes filling with awe, Mable recognized her wasp for certain. Not two meters away from us did it hover. "It's you. I've been looking for you. I wanted to ask you a question."

"I do not know you," replied the wasp. "I do not make it a habit to converse with those outside the hive. Too dangerous. Far too dangerous. I will not answer you should you attempt to ask me your question. And if you try to find me again, I promise you this, I will sting you until you leave me alone."

The threatening insect turned then and flew away deeper into the forest before Mable could say her piece. She stood, collected her branch, and placed the flycatcher on a tuft of soft flower. "Dartmouth," she said, "please hold this branch and watch the flycatcher's vitals. I think I'm just up ahead there with the bees right now, is that correct?"

"Yes, we have now reached the moment in which we discover the naive bees."

"Then I still have time." Mable walked intently in the direction of her stinging fate.

14

So we came to it. Mable could see her former self awaiting my delivery of the naive bee honey in the clearing. She reached down and felt around in the dark until she found a hand-sized stone. She wound up to pitch this stone toward the wasp which she could just barely make out hovering frantically here and there amongst the trees where past Mable would soon be walking. She was about to throw, her aim on the insect undeniable—

"Mable, wait," spoke a familiar voice in the brush just a few steps from us. The child's face could be seen through a pale mist – another self – another, third Mable – tired – thinner than she should have been – but still resilient all the same.

Our Mable dropped her stone making that small sound we had ignored earlier on our journey. "You're… me. What are you doing here, Mable?"

"Same thing as you, Mable," replied the ghostly third version of herself. "Hi, Dartmouth. Hi, Ms. Flycatcher. It's good to see you both. I know it's been a while. But, I promise, I'm coming back to save you… Wait, that still hasn't happened yet." She seemed confused and convicted all at once. "I've still got more steps to retrace. Right."

"What are you talking about, Mable," said Mable. "I've gotta stop myself from getting stung. And then this whole time loop can close and we can go home without getting anyone else hurt."

"No," replied her other self. "You're wrong. Things go better if you do get stung. That's the trick of things. The wasp was coming for this hive one day — one way or another. You were never gonna stop it intentionally. Some things can't be reasoned or bargained with. Some things just need to be left alone. Your getting stung right now is the only thing that stops the wasp from destroying those bees… and those bees are really important. Their survival in this time is critical to the continued shape and existence of reality as we know it. Without them…" the third Mable sniffed back a tear. "Without those bees, everything falls apart. Trust me on this, I've been there. That's what I mean when I say I'm doing the same thing as you. I'm also trying to correct a mistake. Only, our first mistake wasn't a mistake at all — getting stung. It's our second mistake

- our attempt to stop the stinging - that's really bad."

"I don't understand," said our Mable. "I've gotta stop it."

"Why," asked the girl from the future. "Look at your hand now, Mable. Do you still even feel pain there anymore?"

Mable raised her hand to look at the marks. Indeed, they were already fading. "Now that you mention it, no. I guess I don't."

"So what's the point of stopping it now? For us it will fade into such a little memory. For the bees, for - well - the multiverse, it will prove to have massive… gargantuan ramifications. Besides, you can skate on water now. That doesn't happen if you stop this."

"Well, gee, if you're putting it that way," Mable peered back at the first version of herself - so unaware of the journey to come - the journey we were now completing. "I guess I'll have to take your word for it, me."

In that moment, past Mable was stung. Past me blew the wasp away from past us and it scampered off back toward the river. And past us disappeared into Nexus.

The third Mable sighed deep relief.

"The Amazon rainforest is a crazy place, huh," said Mable one.

"We're still seeing it in the river of time," replied Mable three. "That's a good thing. But, yeah, it was definitely crazier for me than I'd realized. Be sure to tell Mama Ao about it, alright? She's gonna love this story. Oh, bring that branch back with you. A-Wee-Wah's gonna love the fruit it makes the first time y'all meet. By the way, Dartmouth, I really do mean it. I'm coming to rescue you. I just have to find a way back to that place. I've gotta keep retracing my steps. But I promise I'll be there. Don't lose heart, okay?"

"O...kay..." My circuits could not at that moment understand the purpose of her words. But now I realize she was talking to this version of me; the me that's trapped in this and several other books narrating to you from beyond my own reality. I dare say it gives me hope to think of this. But how long must I wait, I wonder. And can our dear girl, Mable, ever actually make it back to me? Only the river of time will tell.

To Be Continued
In
Quantum Mable
And
The Super Volcano

If you would like to research the science facts contained within this book, below is a list of non-fiction options for further reading:

Finwise, M. Quantum Physics for Kids. Independently published. 2026.

Montgomery, S. Journey of the Pink Dolphins: An Amazon Quest. Chelsea Green. 2009.

Da Silva, R.C., et al. Nature's Tiny Gatekeepers: How Stingless Bees Keep Enemies Out. Frontiers for Young Minds. 2025

Anthony, W. Corpse Flower (Gross Life Cycles). Enslow Pub Inc. 2021.

Lisa, C. Amazonian Royal Flycatcher Handbook. Independently published. 2026.

Sumner, S. Endless Forms: The Secret World of Wasps. Harper. 2022.

About the Author

c.b.strul is author of The Ancient Ones, CONNECTIVITY, and Papillon IV, as well as the Quantum Mable series of chapter books. He is founder of Odom's Library, a private and independent publishing house that focuses primarily on works of science fiction.

He lives in Los Angeles, California with his wife Madison, their extended family, and four sweet pug doggies.